The Flight of the Magic Clog

D0418257

First published 1979 by Hamish Hamilton Children's Books Ltd.
First published in Fontana Lions 1980
by William Collins Sons & Co Ltd
14 St James's Place, London SW1

Text copyright © 1979 by John Noakes
Illustrations copyright © 1979 by Toni Goffe
Printed in Italy
by G. Canale & C. S.p.A. - Turin

CONDITIONS OF SALE

This book is sold subject to the condition that it shall not,
by way of trade or otherwise, be lent, re-sold, hired out or
otherwise circulated without the publisher's prior consent
in any form of binding or cover other than that in which it
is published and without a similar condition including this
condition being imposed on the subsequent purchaser.

JOHN NOAKES
The Flight of the Magic Clog

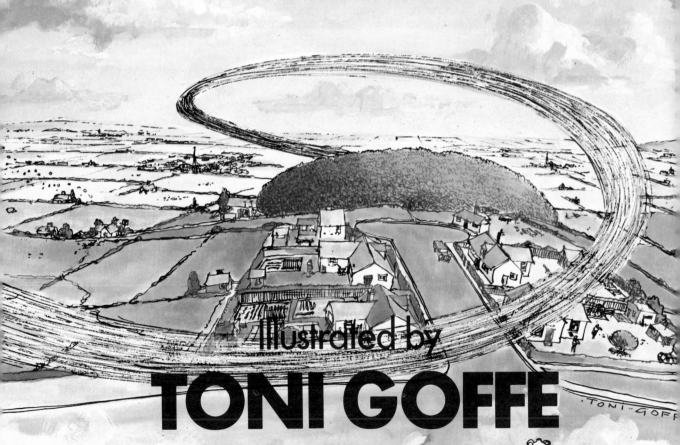

Illustrated by
TONI GOFFE

FONTANA · LIONS

INTRODUCTION

The real John Noakes started life at a place called Sun Wood Avenue, at the bottom of which lay Sun Woods, and beyond that, Bluebell Woods. The avenue was just below Stone Chair at Cross Roads, in the village of Shelf – all strange names that almost seem to have slipped out of a fairy story.

Of course, every fairy story has to have a story teller. Mine lived across the avenue in the house opposite and kept chickens. He was known to me as Mr Brook, but to Mrs Brook – well, she just called him "Fred". He was a large, kind, warm-hearted Yorkshireman with a heart of gold and a voice like velvet, who could tell stories as easily as birds can fly. To me, as a little boy, he never seemed to change – always wearing the same flat hat, suit and waistcoat, and always smoking the same tobacco in his pipe.

Every day I'd walk across to see Mr Brook. Always I would end up sitting beside him, waiting for a story.

"What shall we do today, lad? Feed the chickens?"

"Yes, all right, but first could I have a story?"

And so would start another adventure about me and my long clogs.

I'd better explain about the clogs because they featured in every one of Mr Brook's stories, and were as real to me as I hope they will be to you.

At the back of my house lay a woodyard with a large shed which, said Mr Brook, was the hiding place of my giant pair of magic wooden clogs. In these clogs Mr Brook took me and my four school friends all over the world chasing the evil international villain, Baron Wilhelm von Doppelganger. There was Mickey, very clever and full of brains, always experimenting and inventing things. He didn't say much, but when he did it was with the observation of a scientist. June, on the other hand, never stopped talking, except to dream up some new recipe. Then Barbara, who was my sweetheart – but there's not much you can say about sweethearts, is there? Except that she was as pretty as a picture and a bit bossy. Finally, there was Eric – my best friend – a large lad, not fat, mind you. Heavy's more the mark, and a bit clumsy with it, but a grand lad nevertheless. In Mr Brook's stories we were always together, off on some flight to fantastic adventure in the magic long clogs.

It goes without saying that these Yorkshire stories have to be read with a Yorkshire accent to get the real flavour. Of course, if you live south of Worksop you'll probably say "I can't do one." If that's what you say, just hark back to what Mr Brook once told me – "It doesn't matter if you don't win. What matters is having a good try." But if you didn't try he'd say "You've nobbut to blame but your'sen."

Every day began a new story, and every story began the same way, with me making my way across the road, ready for anything, and lifting my hand to knock on that enchanted door . . .

· ERIC · JUNE · MICKEY · Mc BROOK · JOHN · BARBARA ·

THE SECRET ORDERS

Knock, knock, tapped my knuckles on the door.

"Who's there?" asked Mrs Brook.

"It's me – John – can I come in?"

Mrs Brook opened the door just like every day, saying "Aye, come on in."

As I went into the kitchen there was half a cold rice pudding waiting to go somewhere – which it did, afterwards being washed down with a glass of Dandelion and Burdock. I said my thanks for the rice pudding, which was as good as ever, and knocked on the front parlour door.

"Are you in, Mr Brook?"

"Aye, lad, come on in," said the deep warm voice of Mr Brook. There he was, as always, sat in his easy chair in the same suit, waistcoat and flat hat, and the same pipe filling the room with a lovely aroma as the smoke curled upwards. He told me once that the tobacco was a secret blend grown specially for him by Tibetan monks on the lower slopes of the Himalayas – and, knowing Mr Brook as well as I did, it must have been so.

I sat myself quietly down on the sofa opposite, resting my elbows on the table between us. Mr Brook was looking out of the window, over the chicken huts, beyond Sun Woods into the distance. He was obviously deep in thought.

"What's up, Mr Brook?" I said, a bit worried.

"This," he answered. He held up a telegram in his left hand, and at the bottom I glimpsed the initials "P.M."

"By gum, is that from the Prime Minister himself?" I asked in awe.

"No, lad, it's from Percy Murgatroyd."

"Oh," I muttered, rather disappointed. "I was hoping we might have reached the top man at last."

Mr Brook's eyes rested with a twinkle on me. He tapped the air between us with his pipe, and said with a knowing smile, "I think we have, John, I think we have."

"How come, Mr Brook? I can't say I've ever heard of this Percy Whatsisname."

"Percy Murgatroyd," said Mr Brook, placing his pipe back in his mouth. "He and I were in Intelligence together during the war. We were great friends and got into a fair number of scrapes too, I can tell you." He chuckled quietly to himself.

"That's all very well, but what's it to do with the telegram?" I asked.

8

"Everything, lad. You see, after the war I took to raising chickens, but Percy stayed on with the Intelligence Branch. Over the years we've still kept in touch. He was a clever chap and worked his way through to the top. Now he's our boss and the new Intelligence Co-ordinator, known only to us as 'P.M.'"

"That sounds like good news," I said. "Up till now the secret orders from the Foreign Office have always been a bit muddled and full of wrong information."

"That, I think," said Mr Brook, "will be coming to an end. In fact, the new secret orders from P.M. should be here shortly, and I've got a feeling we'll soon be off again after HIM!"

"Him? Oh, you mean Wicked Willie. Has he been at it again?"

Mr Brook drew deeply on his pipe and blew the smoke gently across the room. He said quietly, "Baron Doppelganger is always at it."

The full name of our dreaded foe was Baron Wilhelm von Doppelganger. Mr Brook, the politest man I every knew, always used his handle and called him "Baron", but to me he was simply "Wicked Willie". Willie was a natural villain and an evil genius with it. He'd risen like a phoenix out of the debris of the war, with a vast amount of looted gold and treasure. With this enormous wealth he'd built up a personal army of rogues and scientists, and a network of secret hide-outs around the world.

His ambition was absolute wealth, total power, and world domination thrown in for good measure, and so far our efforts had done no more than throw a temporary spanner in his works. On many occasions I'd said he was a bit like a chameleon, because whenever we had him cornered he just seemed to disappear and dissolve into the background. Rumour had it that his great-grandad was a gun-fighter in the days of the Wild West, and took part in the last shoot-out on Boot Hill. So I suppose, coming from stock like that, it was difficult to be good.

"Ah, here he comes now," said Mr Brook.

"Who? Wicked Willie?" I asked in a panic.

"No, don't be daft, it's Police Constable Harker on his bike with secret orders."

I looked out of the window and saw our local bobby pedalling like mad down the road, waving a large envelope.

"Now then," said Mr Brook, "you'd better round up your friends and we'll all meet in woodyard in five minutes by the clogs, 'cause I think we've a job to do for P.M. Oh, and by the way," he added as an after-thought, "bring a feather pillow."

I called on Mickey, who lived next door. I knew he was in because of the wispy trails of smoke and steam escaping from the open window.

"Oh dear, another experiment," I thought, and it was.

I found Mickey, his glasses steamed up, in the middle of a maze of strange-looking apparatus, trying to work out a new formula. Various coloured liquids and chemicals were bubbling, boiling and gurgling their way up, down and around corkscrewed glass tubing, odd-shaped bottles and other paraphernalia.

"I'll see you in the woodyard in a minute," said Mickey, after I'd told him about the trip. "But first I'm going to run an electric current through this lot to see what'll happen."

I had a funny feeling about what might happen – and I was right! There was a muffled explosion as I went to see June, my next friend. She was clever too, but her skill lay in the oven. Her baking was famous throughout the village, as was her tendency to talk. Once she started it was difficult to get a word in edgeways.

"That's the trouble with being brainy and wanting to become a scientist – you have to blow yourself up a few times to succeed," June chattered as she took the newly-baked bread out of the oven. "Imagine," she went on, without even stopping to take a breath, "what would happen if my loaves went bang every time I baked! I mean to say . . ."

"Just a moment," I interrupted, firmly but politely, "if you'll get the sandwiches ready, I'll go and pick up Eric."

I left quickly, June still muttering away ten to the dozen, and made my way to Cross Roads, by the woodyard. I found my best friend Eric at his dad's petrol station, struggling to put a large wheel back on a lorry.

"At least Eric won't blow himself up," I thought.

Eric asked his mum if he could come with us, and she said yes, but he had to be back by teatime – and what did he want a feather pillow for?

"Mind you, it does seem a bit odd," said Eric as we crossed to the woodyard.

At that moment Mr Brook came into view, walking up the hill from Mrs Grazby's shop. He was laden with tins of treacle, and Barbara (my sweetheart) was giving him a hand.

Feather pillows! Tins of treacle! Whatever next?

"Stop gawping, you two, and give us a hand!" said Mr Brook.

We took some tins to lighten their load. I asked Barbara if she was coming along.

"Just you try and stop me!" said Barbara. "Someone's got to look after you and see that you don't get into any more trouble."

I didn't say anything, as Eric overheard the whole conversation and grinned at me. I scowled back at him, and blushed bright red. Well, there are things a sweetheart can and can't say when there are folk present, and Eric can hear a whisper at forty paces.

We all arrived at the woodyard gate, which was open. Waiting by the sign that said "KEEP OUT, BY ORDER" – painted very neatly, apart from a few paint runs, by Eric and me – were Mickey and P.C. Harker. The Police Constable was still puffing a bit from his pedalling, but at our approach he took a deep breath, which expanded his chest to full official capacity, and stated, "I'll just check your passes on entering this secret establishment."

"Seems a bit daft to me," Eric said as we filed through. "He knows who we are, and that we're the only ones allowed in woodyard. If you ask me, he's getting a bit too fussy these days."

"Nobody asked you," chipped in Barbara, hard on our heels. "It's his attention to detail and dedication to duty that makes him the best police-man utside of Halifax."

Eric took a kick at an old chunk of wood lying about, and moved ahead quickly. Once out of earshot, he felt brave enough to say, "By gum, I'm fair glad she's your sweetheart, not mine!"

At this point he looked around worried – very worried – in case she'd overheard again. But no, Barbara was trotting quite happily with the others up to the woodshed door.

On arrival, Mr Brook reached into his waistcoat pocket and brought out a very strangely shaped key, which he placed into an even stranger-looking lock. It was one of Mickey's inventions, which he claimed was un-pickable, with dials and levers on the outside and a clockwork motor and pulleys on the inside. The workings whirred away almost silently, while Mr Brook moved levers up and down and from side to side through the correct sequence.

Suddenly the whirring stopped and the lock clicked twice and sprang open. Slowly the two doors drew apart.

They rumbled along their tracks, revealing the inside of the woodshed, whose darkness was punctured only by a shaft of light which slid down from the skylight above. The draught caused by the sudden inrush of air sucked and swirled the sawdust up into the darkness, only to find itself trapped and shimmering in the shaft of light, which seemed to transform itself into a pillar of gold.

I never did understand how the sawdust always found its way into that light, but as my eyes travelled down the golden column, they were met by a sight equalled only by that of a pot of gold at the foot of a rainbow. It was always a moment of magic for me, and no matter how many times I'd stood, stared and seen the same vision, there were always those few seconds when I just couldn't move, because there they were, bathed in sunlight, the long clogs, side by side and almost as big as a single decker bus. By gum, they were a grand sight – and strange, too, because they somehow made distance shrink and time stand still.

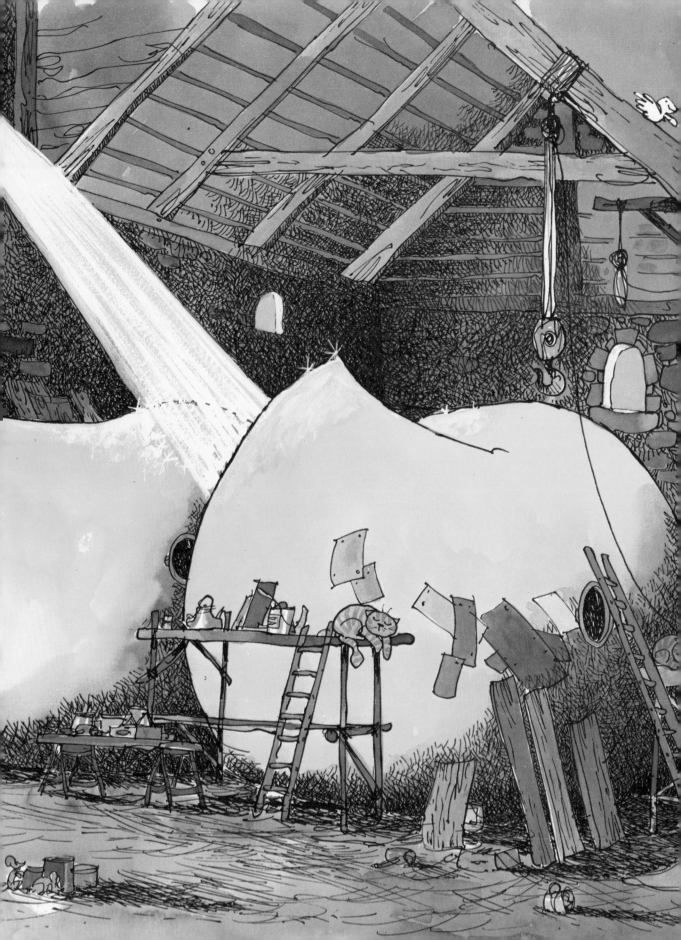

"You'll have to go in the right clog, as I haven't quite finished repairing the other," said P.C. Harker. So we all put our shoulders against the right clog and pushed. It slid gently over the sawdust and out into the morning air. We clambered aboard. Eric and I stowed the feather pillows and tins of treacle down in the toe. June was taking the sandwiches out of her satchel and packing them away in the bread bin, at the same time giving Mickey a right earful about how *her* loaves didn't go bang in the oven!

Mr Brook signed for the secret orders and P.C. Harker handed them over. Sitting down, he quietly pored over them.

Meanwhile, I asked Mickey – who was sporting a few new pieces of sticking plaster – how his experiment had gone.

"Not so bad, but it's early days yet, as I haven't tested it," said Mickey, taking a bottle out of his pocket and giving it a shake. He smiled at me mysteriously, and replaced the bottle.

Mr Brook looked up at us all: "Right then, we're off to the north coast of Germany. Could be a tough assignment for us this time."

"Aye, and it could get a bit sticky too," whispered Eric, pointing to the tins of treacle.

P.C. Harker said he'd be waiting for us when we got back, and wished us luck.

Mickey set the compass and the altimeter. Mr Brook took over the controls and, with the flick of a switch, started the engine in the sole of the clog. A gentle hum sang through the wooden clog which soon disappeared as we rose silently above the woodyard. With a surge of power we slid forward, leaving Sun Woods far behind in a matter of seconds, climbing at the same time and reaching for the sky.

ENEMY COAST AHEAD

Mickey, who was the navigation expert, quickly worked out a course for Bridlington Harbour, a good landmark from which to start our journey across the North Sea. The clog banked slightly as Mr Brook turned to head on to the new course. As we sped through the sky an uneasy calm, before the excitement to come, was felt throughout the whole of the clog.

Mr Brook felt it too. I could tell from the way he fiddled with the gold chain attached to his waistcoat, on the end of which hung his pocket watch. Finally, he hauled it out, pressed the winder, and the lid sprang open with a click.

"As we've a moment or two to spare," announced Mr Brook, "I'll tell you about our new Co-ordinator, P.M."

We all listened intently as he told us about the new man at the top, and their wartime adventures together.

At the end, Eric said thoughtfully, "Wasn't it a Percy Murgatroyd who used to run the chip shop at Cross Roads a long time ago?"

"That was good observation, Eric," said Mr Brook, "As a matter of fact it was. In the early days, when we were building John's clogs, the fish and chip shop was his cover. He's gone a long way since then . . . But I think from now on we'll have radio silence."

Eric was just about to make another observation about the fact that we hadn't used the radio yet, but Barbara shushed him up: so he shrugged his shoulders and volunteered to stand watch as he always did. He put on one of Mr Brook's old cast-off flat hats (back to front of course), pulled an old pair of flying goggles over his eyes, and wrapped a scarf tightly around his neck.

He'd complained once that it was a bit draughty with your head sticking up above the clog, Thus clad, Eric took a telescope out of its case and made his way down to the hatch in the toe to keep watch. Mr Brook checked over the workings of the instruments and controls and went down in the engine well to make sure that the magnetic field coil was in a constant flow relative to the anti-gravity drive what's-er-name or something or other – at least, that's what I think he was doing.

June, for once, was remaining silent and getting the sandwiches ready, while Barbara lit the wick of the paraffin stove.

"Would you like a cup of tea?" she asked.

"Um, please," I replied, but I don't know why she asked me, as she always made one for Mr Brook. He said it settled him and made him think more clearly, and I'm sure he was right.

All this time I was checking that the right equipment was aboard, stowed away and tied down. Suddenly, I remembered Eric's braces. I crawled forward to the toe of the clog, tapped Eric on the knee and shouted up, "Have you brought your braces?" There was a slight pause before the windswept head of Eric came down into view. "'Course I have," he snorted. "If I hadn't, my pants would have fallen down, wouldn't they!"

I didn't say anything, and just smiled as Eric's head disappeared back up into the cold air. I nearly said that they could have been held up by string, but thought better of it. Eric's braces had come in useful quite a few times, and I'd no wish to offend him.

Inside the clog, we had hardly taken a bite out of June's sandwiches when Eric called out, "Bridlington Harbour's in sight." Mr Brook told Mickey where we were heading for, and he checked over the charts of the North Sea and German coast, drawing lines here, there and everywhere, using a pair of compasses for measuring distances and muttering things

to himself – like "Magnetic variation, compass deviation," and other strange utterances. Finally, he called out a course of 94° for Mr Brook to steer on the compass.

Once on the new course Mr Brook opened the throttle and we fairly shifted along while Bridlington disappeared behind us, soon becoming nought but a dot on the horizon. Mr Brook handed me a message to pass down to Eric, explaining what next to keep his eyes open for, and when that was delivered we quickly sat down to finish our sandwiches and tea.

After he finished his cup of tea Mr Brook filled his pipe, pressing the tobacco gently down into the bowl as only an expert can. Then, shielding the spluttering match with his hand, he drew on it quickly with short puffs until the top of the pipe bowl glowed bright red and the smoke swirled around.

With the pipe-lighting ceremony over he said, "Right then! If you'll gather round I'll brief you on these." He held up the secret orders.

"At the moment agents all over the world are having a big sweep, trying to flush out Baron Doppelganger and his cronies, but so far they have met with little success. P.M.'s had a report from one of his spies that the Baron has a large, well-camouflaged ammunition factory – just HERE." Mr Brook placed his finger on the chart over a spit of land jutting out from the coast. "Now this," he said, "used to be a small isolated fishing village, but because the harbour has silted up over the years, the village has just died a natural death. It's nearly in ruins, and only a few houses are still occupied.

"Now," Mr Brook went on, "P.M. sent in his secret agents disguised as tourists. They certainly weren't made welcome by the 'locals', who turned out to be an unsavoury bunch – obviously members of the Baron's gang. Even so, the agents checked through the village thoroughly, poked around in every nook and cranny, and found nothing. In fact, they don't believe the factory exists. But P.M. has a funny feeling that it does, and he says that if anyone can find it, we can."

"I don't see why they don't send in the Army to capture the villains and village in one fell swoop," I said.

"Ah," Mr Brook explained, "if that happened all they might end up with would be a few prisoners, but no factory – and the factory is the main object of our mission. Mind you, if we don't spot it from the air, it'll mean going down to land in the Baron's territory."

That last statement sent a shiver down my spine, and when Eric shouted, "Action stations! Enemy coast ahead!" I nearly jumped out of my skin.

On hearing Eric's warning, Mr Brook knocked out his pipe and took the clog up into the base of the clouds for cover, slowing down at the same time. We cleared up the tea things and rushed to our various Action positions. I took a couple of sandwiches forward for Eric, whose teeth were chattering a bit by now, and told him about the secret orders.

"Can anyone see a small island below?" shouted Mickey, still checking the charts.

"Of course I can, it's just down there," reported Barbara. And when we all looked through the swirling mist of the clouds, it was.

We rose higher into the cloud because now, more than ever, secrecy had to be maintained at all costs. Mickey said the distance from the island to the fishing village was fifty miles. Mr Brook checked the weather forecast chart, which P.M. had thoughtfully included with the secret orders, and it showed cloud covering this part of Germany.

"We'll have to fly blind through cloud from now on," said Mr Brook, and he and Mickey set about working out the course, speed, and time of arrival. After a bit of muttering and measuring came the instruction – nothing more than "Hang on to your hats!"

The sudden surge of speed caught Eric unawares and he sat down with a thud – right on top of June's sandwiches.

I saved Eric from a second collision with the sandwiches by holding tightly to his braces. He put the sandwiches away. Then he turned to me and smiled. I smiled back. No words were needed – we both knew what a lucky escape it had been.

As though the smile was a cue, the clog came to a halt, hovering and swinging slightly in the breeze. The cloud rolled over the edge of the clog, slowly filling it up.

"At this moment we are exactly above the fishing village," announced Mickey, wiping the cloud from his glasses with his tie.

Mr Brook's watch-lid clicked open and he murmured, "Made good time so far." He sat there quite still for a moment, gazing at the watch face, deep in thought, as though searching for an answer to a question.

"Now then, let's see." He went on murmuring – not to anyone in particular, in fact more to himself. "Can't fly below the clouds or we'll be spotted, and I reckon a reconnaissance over the outlying district might just bring something to light. Any ideas?" he enquired, looking up.

"It seems obvious to me," piped up Barbara. "Why not try out that camera Mickey's always messing about with?"

"A good idea," said Mr Brook. "Quick, lads, get out the high speed camera."

Eric and I unhooked a long hollow pole from the wall of the clog while Mickey lifted the box Brownie camera gingerly from its case. Strapped to it was a large meccano clockwork motor which drove a series of gears and pulleys which, in their turn, pushed and pressed various levers.

"I think I can safely say at last," said Mickey, "that I've overcome the problem of turning the film in the camera and pressing the button at the same time."

"I should blooming well hope so," thundered Eric. "Last time we had ten pictures come out and they were all printed one on top of each other, like an Ordnance Survey map with hiccups."

"Now come on, you lot, don't waste time," said Mr Brook. "Tie that piece of string to the On-Off Lever and lower the pole and camera over the side."

Eric was a good worker, and after a few moments he peered down the hollow pole and said, "It's all ready now, Mr Brook. The pole's sticking out of the cloud, 'cause I can see the harbour below and the camera's pointing down in the right direction."

"Good! Everyone hold on tight! We'll do a high speed run up the river!" warned Mr Brook. "John, when I say 'Right!' pull the string to the camera's motor!"

The wooden clog creaked with the strain of the sudden acceleration, emptying itself of cloud in a matter of moments. Mr Brook, his eyes trained on the second hand of his pocket watch, suddenly called out, "Right!"

I pulled the string and just hoped the clockwork motor was doing its job below while above, we three lads hung on to the pole for all we were worth to keep it pointing downwards.

There was no way of knowing what was happening below, but I did notice that Mickey's fingers were crossed as he hung on to the top of the pole. After what seemed an eternity came the call "Run completed!" and Mr Brook slipped his pocket watch back into his waistcoat, saying, "If Mickey's camera's worked, and my timing was right, we should have some good pictures of the landscape below."

The clog slowed down and shuddered to a halt.

"About here should be safe enough," said Mr Brook, and once more we were enveloped by cloud and silence.

We lifted the pole back into the clog, relieved to find the camera still attached. After a quick check Mickey handed the film to Mr Brook, who disappeared down into the workshop. Actually, the workshop was a large

old wardrobe which I'd bought for fifty pence from the secondhand shop down by the Sunday School. Eric thought at the time that it was a good buy and that I had definite possibilities as an antique dealer, though he did change his tune a bit when we found we couldn't get it in through my front door. But after P.C. Harker had gone to work on it, unscrewing the back and shaping the corners, it fastened up against the side of the clog a treat. So it became our workshop, and very useful too for the odd running repair which we had to do now and again. Also, with no trouble at all, we'd turned it into a darkroom as well.

While Mr Brook sloshed developing liquids around, I told Eric how Mickey had had his fingers crossed.

"That's nowt, I had everything crossed – including my eyes!" he replied.

Mr Brook opened the wardrobe door and came out holding ten dripping wet pictures.

"Come and have a look at these!" he said, laying them out on the floor, edge to edge in a long line.

"By heck, them's grand, aren't they!" exclaimed Eric. We all gazed at them, and they were. It was like looking at a picture that had been stretched. It was all long and thin, and you could clearly see the fishing village and inland for about a mile, with the river winding its way through the middle like a gleaming strip of quicksilver.

"Right, let's see what we can make out of this lot," said Mr Brook as we knelt down around the long line of photographs, "and also see what is there, before we discover what is not there."

"How do you mean?" said June. "How can you discover something isn't there when it's not there, 'cause if it's not there it can't have been there, and if it can't have been there it must be somewhere else, and we don't have pictures of somewhere else, do we?"

By the time she finished all that, there was the most silent silence I've ever heard. Eric broke it with a whisper, "I think she's gone cracked like the crust on her bread!"

But Mr Brook was kinder. "No, I meant discovering if the ammunition factory is or isn't there. You see, it may be there, well camouflaged, looking as though it's not there: but if it's not there, it may look as though . . ." His voice trailed off. "I'll tell you what," he said, "let's study the pictures step by step to see if it is or it isn't."

At this point, Eric dug his hands deep into his pockets, which were always bulging with various bits and pieces, and out of one of them he took a magnifying glass and started to study each picture closely.

"As I see it," said Mickey, "here's the fishing village as described by P.M.'s agents. The harbour's silted up, and not much is left standing. There's a car parked down there, and someone's riding a bike, but there's certainly nothing big enough for a factory. I think I can safely say that."

"I'd say that looks a bit of a problem," I muttered.

"You could say that," agreed Eric, still peering away.

"I just *did* say that . . ."

But all this was cut short by Mickey, who went on, "Inland, south of the river, is low-lying marshland, and that's all. On the north side the ground is higher, with a few fields and moorland beyond. A road runs along by the river, as does a hedge – and there's a small wood half-way along, quite close to the river. But I can't see a building hidden inside."

Eric looked up from his magnifying glass and said, "You know, the pictures are so clear you can even see the daffodils in the fields, but . . ."

There were no "buts" about it, because Barbara's head turned and she looked sternly at Eric. "They don't just grow in England, you know. Daffodils grow in Germany too."

Eric rose to his full height, or at least as high as he could while still kneeling. He stuck his thumbs in his braces, which was always a sign that a powerful statement was about to be issued, and looked Barbara straight in the eye – bravery in itself.

"If you'd just let me finish, I was going to say that there are daffodils in the fields but none in the woods. And if they grow in Sun Woods, why don't they grow in these German woods?"

"Um, aye . . . that's very interesting," said Mr Brook, viewing the wood through Eric's magnifying glass, "and very odd, too. I think that needs investigating."

Mr Brook looked up and made the immediate decision, "Camouflage nets out! Prepare to land!"

"By heck, I should have said nowt," muttered Eric, as we pulled the rolled-up net out of its locker.

"On second thoughts," he said loudly, "Wicked Willie and his gang might have picked all the daffodils. Did you hear that, Mr Brook?" But Mr Brook didn't.

Barbara did, though, and simply said, "Don't be silly, Wicked Willie wouldn't go around picking flowers."

"No, but I bet his prisoners do," muttered Eric gloomily, thinking the worst and hoping to put off the moment of landing.

But that moment arrived almost unnoticed. We were so busy tugging and tussling with the net that we didn't even feel the clog drop like a stone from the clouds above to the water below. Due to Mr Brook's expert handling of the controls, the only sign of our arrival was a ripple or two on the water.

THE SECRET FACTORY

Mr Brook and the girls jumped ashore with ropes to pull us in close and moor us to a couple of small bushes, while we lads briskly unrolled the netting, covering over the clog. After a couple of minutes of hard work weaving in rushes, clumps of grass and bits of bushes, it was difficult to tell where the bank finished and the clog started. It was so well camouflaged, in fact, that at one point Eric was trying to get down a large fox hole thinking it was the entrance into the clog through the net.

"Done a fair job there," said Mr Brook, climbing back into the clog. The rest of us stood admiring our handiwork, except June, who was nervously nibbling one of her sandwiches, which she often did on these dangerous occasions.

Suddenly she choked, spluttering and pointing wildly.

"What's up, love?" asked Eric, thumping her on the back, "A crumb gone down the wrong way?"

"No, no," she croaked, "There's a man on a bike coming down the road, and he's got a gun!"

That was it. We didn't even look to see if it was true. One moment we were standing on the river bank. The next, we were tumbling head first through the entrance hole in the net and on to the floor of the clog. For once, strangely, Eric wasn't last. It was Barbara and June who brought up the rear. Barbara looked at Eric and me, all tangled up, and said meaningfully, "I thought it was supposed to be women and children first!"

"Well, to-day," said Eric, still trying to untangle his head from under my legs, "to-day I come under the heading of 'children'!"

Now that the knocking had stopped inside, the squeaking outside seemed to get louder and louder until it was almost on top of us. But then it passed and gradually disappeared into the distance.

Mr Brook gingerly poked his head out through the camouflage net, parted a clump of grass and looked around. "Good," he said, "the danger's passed now and he's off down the road. Anybody see anything suspicious?"

Five other heads joined his and peered out. Our eyes scanned from left to right and back again. I certainly couldn't see anything out of the ordinary.

"Nothing different from the photos," declared Mickey. "That wood over there is just – "

"That wood," interrupted Mr Brook, "there's something about that wood. It's not just that there aren't any flowers there, as Eric's already said. It's something else, but I just can't put my finger on it."

"I'm not surprised," said Eric, "it's at least a hundred metres away!"

We chuckled at this, but it didn't amuse Barbara, because when Mr Brook asked for two volunteers for the scouting party she quickly pointed at Eric and me and ordered, "You and you!" The smiles disappeared from our faces.

"Right! Follow me," said Mr Brook, leading the way.

We crossed the river bank, pausing only to make sure that no more squeaky bikes were coming, and dashed across the road to take cover in the hedgerow.

"What now, Mr Brook?" I asked when the two of us caught him up.

"Along the hedge till we're opposite the wood, but if you see anyone coming," warned Mr Brook, "dive straight through it!"

"It looks prickly to me," moaned Eric.

"Better that than being taken prisoner," I said.

Eric agreed. Anything was better than that!

Bending double, we moved off, coming to a halt when we thought we should be opposite the wood.

"I'll just look over the hedge to see how the land lies," I said, trying to appear brave about it all. Cautiously I peered over the top. We'd stopped in the right place. Just a few metres away was the small wood.

"See anything?" whispered Eric.

"Not much," I whispered back. "One wood looks very much like any other. Hang on a minute, though – there's a sort of cart-track leading from the wood to where we are."

Eric's curiosity got the better of him. He stood up and joined me, leaning on the hedge.

"You're right," he said, "it comes up to the hedge here, and . . ."

He got no further in his observation because at that point the hedge started moving. It just seemed to swing away, leaving the two of us flabbergasted.

Eric was the first to croak, "It's alive. These people have a secret weapon, live hedges! They could take over the world!"

"Hang on a moment," said Mr Brook calmly, "hedges don't just move like that without good reason."

"A secret weapon is a good enough reason for me," said Eric.

"John, pull that hedge back!" ordered Mr Brook.

I pulled delicately on a small twig, trying not to look as if I expected to be taken prisoner by the hedge. To my relief it swung back silently to join up with the rest.

"Eh, I don't know!" laughed Mr Brook. "You two are daft halfpennies. All it is is a gate, and the hedge has grown over it!"

He put his hand inside the hedge, felt about, and suddenly said, "Hello! There's something not quite right here!"

The smile left his face as he fiddled around a bit more and said seriously, "That's cunning! This hedge didn't just grow along the gate, it was trained. Obviously someone doesn't want it to be known that there's a way in."

He thought for another moment, then said, "As that's the case, in we go. We'll take cover behind those trees on each side of the track."

Mr Brook swung open the hedge and we squeezed through. Then we sprinted up the track. The early panic of the moving hedge had certainly given a boost to Eric's legs, because he fairly streaked ahead, leaving Mr Brook and me behind. As I raced along after Eric I couldn't help noticing something rather odd about the track; it suddenly came to an abrupt halt between two trees and went no further into the wood.

It was odder still when Eric reached that point because he, too, came to an abrupt halt and went no further. He seemed to freeze in mid-air and hang there for a second. Then, as if in slow motion, he fell backwards with a moan.

"What's up, Eric?" I asked when I reached him.

"Mortally wounded, I am," he just managed to gurgle.

"What on earth with?" I queried, looking round to see who or what was the mortal wounder.

"It's the invisible hand. It struck me down!" Eric burbled.

"With live hedges and invisible hands," I said, "it'll be ghosts from the haunted wood next!"

That was the last straw for poor Eric. His eyes rolled with terror, a moan came from between his lips and his legs got strength from an unknown source, because with one bound he was up and hurtling towards the clog with feet hardly touching the ground.

Now panic is a bit like measles. It's catching at times, and I caught a bit of it from Eric. I was about to run after him when Mr Brook said "Just a moment!" and reached out to where the seemingly invisible hand had stopped Eric in his tracks.

"Have a feel of that, then!" said Mr Brook.

"How can I have a feel of it if there's nothing there?"

"No, go on," he urged.

Nervously I slid my hand forward into the empty space. Suddenly it stopped, as it came in contact with – nothing; or at least it must have been something because nothing wouldn't have stopped it.

"That's what I couldn't put my finger on," said Mr Brook.

"I'm not surprised, because it's not there," I said, still astonished.

"No, it's not that," Mr Brook replied. "It's the trees! They don't move in the breeze. Everything's beginning to tumble into place!" The flat of his hand thrust forward into the empty space and a definite thump was heard. He got quite excited.

"I think we've discovered the secret factory!" he said.

The penny that had dropped for Mr Brook certainly hadn't dropped for me. I was flummoxed and still trying to puzzle it out.

"How can we have, Mr Brook?" I whispered back, "I can see right into the wood and there's nothing but trees."

"No, lad, you're looking at a masterpiece of painting," he replied. "It's just an optical illusion."

"But these two trees here definitely stick out," I said, puzzled, "and have real branches."

"Nay, John, it's not that you can't see the wood for the trees, it's that you can't see the trees for the plastic – because that's what they are, just plastic moulded trees, branches an' all, and in between them is a huge mural painted on the walls!"

The penny finally dropped, like a lead balloon.

"By gum!" I muttered. "That Wicked Willie must be a genius!"

"I'm beginning to think the Baron isn't as clever as we first thought," said Mr Brook. "A proper genius would have planted real trees, and if that had been done we might not have bothered with the wood at all."

He removed his flat hat for the first time that day and gave the top of his head a good scratch. When he did that it was always the sign of deep thoughts and the drawing up of plans. Finally the flat hat plopped back on his head and he said "Right! That's that! I think I know what's to be done."

With that we followed in Eric's footsteps, beating a hasty retreat to the clog.

PRISONER OF WAR

The orders soon came thick and fast.

No sooner had we laid all the things out on the river bank than Mr Brook emerged from the depths of the clog wearing a beret, paint-spattered smock, and sporting a little stick-on moustache. He was a master of disguises and this was a good one. He looked just like one of those artist fellows as he stepped ashore.

"Are we at Battle Stations now?" asked Eric, whose sense of the dramatic was even greater than before.

Mr Brook faced his troops and said, "You're absolutely right, Eric, Battle Stations it is! Barbara and June will stay behind – one to keep a look out and the other to cut open the top of each pillow. The rest of you, put on these berets," he said, handing them round. "Pick up your paint brushes and treacle tins, and follow me!"

With that, Mr Brook set off down the road.

"But we're in full view of anybody who might be watching," protested Mickey as we followed. Mr Brook nodded.

"We've got to act as if we're painters coming to touch up the camouflage here and there. But what we're really going to do is paint that factory with treacle from tip to root."

"Like a giant treacle pudding," said Mickey, still puzzled.

Somehow, once Battle Stations had been called, we were on our toes, alert and afeared of nothing. We marched through the hidden hedge gate as if we'd always known it was there, down the track and round to the back of the camouflaged secret factory.

As we parked the tins down in a pile, Mr Brook said, "Right, Mickey and I will climb one of those trees and start on the roof. John, you follow and paint the top of the sides – and Eric, you stay down here and do all round the bottom!"

I followed them both up till I could just reach the top. Then, brush in hand, I dipped it into the treacle and set about painting while Eric did the same below. But we had to come down again to help Eric when one of the factory workers trapped him against the newly painted door.

Back at the clog, things hadn't been quite so funny and, unknown to us, a small drama was unfolding. Barbara, who was not known for sitting about twiddling her thumbs, had grown restless keeping a look out, and decided to see what we were up to. She'd set off down the road without even checking that all was clear when a huge open car drew up alongside her. The driver was a large man wearing a leather trench-coat and hat – in fact, everything about him was large, even his evil eye, which glared down at her with curiosity through his monocle. It was the Baron – Wicked Willie himself!

"Good morning," he said, raising his hat sarcastically.

Barbara – being Barbara – just ignored him and kept on walking.

Now the Baron was obviously not used to being ignored, and he drew alongside her again, screaming, "You! Stop!"

Certainly Barbara wasn't used to being screamed at. She turned, looked him straight in his monocle and said icily, "Mr Brook says I shouldn't talk to strange men, so GO AWAY!"

The Baron's monocle dropped from his eye.

"MISTER BROOK!" he said in a tone of voice that sent a shiver down Barbara's spine. "That man is the scourge of my life!"

"We all are," said Barbara bravely, but putting her foot in it even more.

A large hand grabbed her by the scruff of her neck and hauled her into the car.

"You must be one of Mr Brook's useless little gang," he shouted. "Well, now you are my prisoner and from you I will get his secrets!"

"All you'll get from me," said Barbara firmly, "is name, rank and bus ticket number."

"By the end of the day," sneered the Baron, "you will be telling me secrets you didn't even know you knew."

With that he put the car into gear and roared off down the road.

Back at the secret factory I was still laughing at Eric, but the laughter was short-lived. The shout of "Enemy approaching!" brought us to our senses.

"Who? What? Where?"

"Get yourselves up here and out of sight!" shouted Mickey from the roof. "And hide."

"What's up?"

"It's Barbara – she's been captured!"

"She's been what?" we cried.

We crouched on the roof and peered over the edge. Sure enough, speeding down the road in a great big open-topped car was Barbara. Sitting next to her and driving the car was a most unpleasant-looking person.

"It's him. It's the Baron," we heard Mr Brook say.

There was Barbara, sitting with arms firmly folded, lips pursed tight and eyebrows knitted together, looking exceedingly angry. At that moment I wasn't quite sure who I felt sorry for – Barbara or the Baron.

Suddenly the tyres screeched as the car turned, banged the hedge gate open and roared down the cart-track, giving two loud honks of the horn. That was obviously a signal because a large door hidden in the factory wall opened and, with a swirl of dust, the car disappeared inside. As quickly as it had opened, the door closed again, dissolving itself into the camouflage once more.

Silence again descended, but it was short-lived because down the road came June, sandwich in hand, running at half speed and talking at full speed. She shouted to Mr Brook that she'd seen the whole occurrence and how disgraceful it was . . . and anything else that came to mind.

She leapt over the hedge like an Olympic hurdler, managing to get through three more sentences before reaching the ground.

Something had to be done, and done quickly. In the heat of the moment Eric and I jumped down, grabbed the sandwich and pushed it into June's mouth. Blissful silence descended for the second time.

We brought June over to hide with us by one of the plastic trees.

"I thought if it worked with my knees it should work with June's talking," said Eric, grinning, "and anyhow, I quite enjoyed doing that!"

June's eyes flashed as she tried to answer, but the sandwich held firm.

We climbed the nearest tree. Once on the roof we lay flat with the others on the only untreacled section.

"I'm not leaving here without my Barbara," I informed everyone.

"That's as maybe, but first we've got to get her out of there," said Mr Brook. "We need a plan."

"I know," I suggested, "we could wait till the car drives out, then jump off the roof into it, overpower the Baron and drive off."

"That sort of stuff only happens in films," said Mr Brook.

"We could always go in through this door," muttered Eric.

"What door?" we cried.

"This one here," he replied, scraping dirt out of a groove with his penknife. "I think it's a sort of trap-door. If we can open it we might be able to get inside the factory."

"Eric, you're a genius!" said Mickey.

"Well, that makes a change," said Eric modestly.

"Right, Eric!" said Mr Brook. "See if your penknife's strong enough to lever it up."

Eric set to work. It was touch and go for a bit, but suddenly the door eased a fraction – just enough to let us get our fingertips underneath. We raised it slowly till Mr Brook was able to slide his tobacco tin into the widening gap and hold the door open. As we peered through the opening an amazing sight appeared before our eyes.

P.M. had been right about his funny feeling, because down below was the secret ammunition factory in full swing. Bombs and shells were moving this way and that along conveyor belts and finally being stacked neatly into piles just beneath us.

"They're even building tanks down that end!" said Mickey.

"And there's Barbara!" I cried.

"Where?"

"Down there by the tanks," I said.

And when we looked, there she was, still sitting in the car. It was parked a little way inside the factory, and the Baron, who had now got out, was obviously discussing her with the Works Manager (at least I think he was the Works Manager because he was all dressed up in a suit and tie).

"Oh heck! Poor Barbara's a prisoner of war now," moaned Eric, to whom even the thought was agony.

"But not for long," said Mr Brook. "I have a plan which, if it works, should get us out of here and away in five minutes – with Barbara, of course."

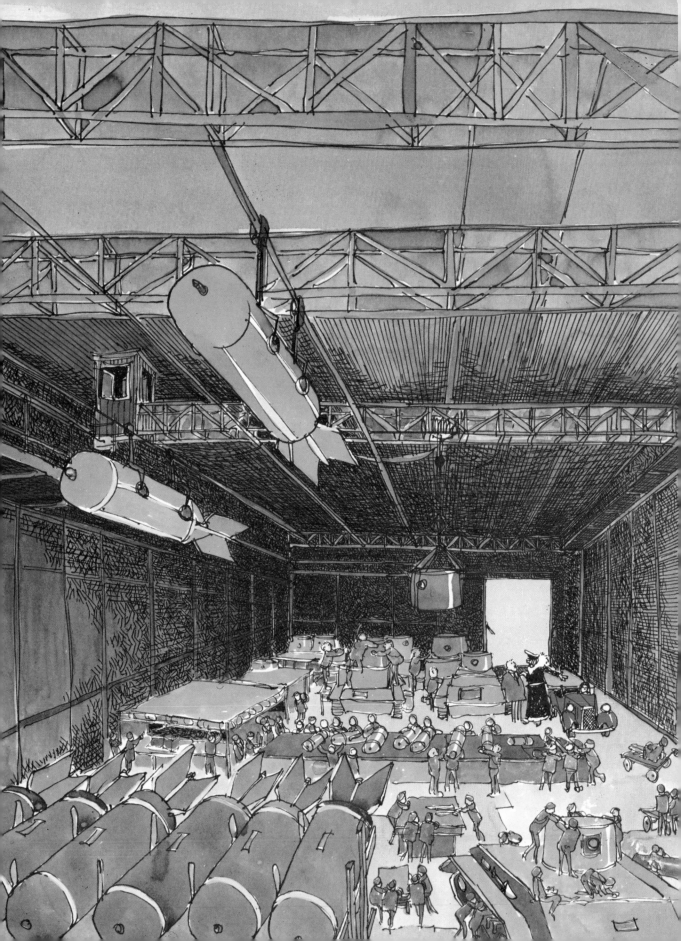

THE ESCAPE

Mr Brook briskly took command.

"Eric, give John your braces."

"That's a funny plan – all that will happen is that my pants will fall down."

"With all that treacle on you there's no chance of that," said Mickey as Eric struggled with his braces.

"Now, this is what we'll do," said Mr Brook. "June, you get all the tins of treacle up on to the roof and start pouring them down the walls. Eric will join you as soon as possible to help and when that's done, both hightail it back to the clog and prepare for immediate take-off."

"What am I going to do first?" asked Eric.

"Attack through the trap-door," said Mr Brook.

"What? . . . By myself? . . . But Mr Brook, it's a big drop to the factory floor."

"Don't be daft, there's a catwalk all the way round, and we're all coming with you," answered Mr Brook.

"There's a giant overhead mobile crane, and it has to be captured," said Mr Brook calmly. "You two commandos are the ones who can do it. Move!"

Eric and I dropped through the trap-door on to the catwalk below, crouched down and surveyed the situation. Mickey and Mr Brook followed close behind.

"Driver. GO!" mouthed Mr Brook, knowing it was a waste of time trying to shout over the din. As he pointed up ahead towards the crane Eric and I moved off on our hands and knees, heading for the driver's cab. We'd worked together so often we knew what had to be done and how to do it. The crane driver was the target and the element was surprise.

Outside the cab door Eric fished about in his pockets for a piece of thick string, while I practised a couple of quick karate chops. When everything was ready I nodded to Eric, who opened the door and, with a yell of "Charge!" we flung ourselves at the driver's seat. In a confusion of arms and legs we crashed to the ground, and it was all over very quickly with two wrists tightly bound together! In the heat of the moment, however, we had failed to notice one thing – the seat was empty! Eric had tied up the first two wrists he came across . . . mine! He apologised and reclaimed his string. I beckoned out of the cab to Mickey and Mr Brook. It was sighs of relief all round when, together again, we closed the door and shut out the noise.

"I think the driver's gone for his tea break," said Eric innocently.

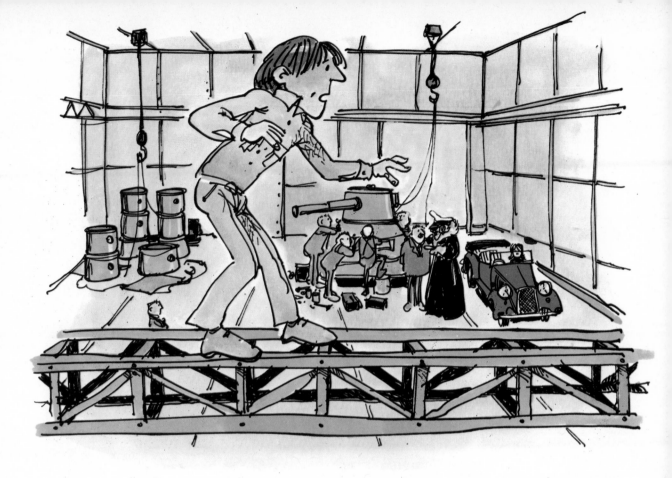

"Let's hope so," said Mr Brook, looking about. "Eric, you go off and help June. Right, Mickey, we haven't much time. You're the mechanical one. Can you work this crane?" His eyes ran over the control levers. "They're all marked with arrows for 'up', 'down' and 'side to side'. No, it shouldn't be too difficult."

While Mickey sorted out which lever did what, Mr Brook looked at me and said, "Now, John! Bravery is more in your line. This is what I want you to do." By the time I'd been briefed Mickey had the monstrous crane moving slowly sideways along its track. The next stage was up to me.

There was no need for words. The others looked across and nodded. I nodded back, slipped out of the cab door and clambered up the side on to the top girder section which spanned the factory floor below. It was a bit like walking along parallel bars in the school gym – only these were moving sideways, which didn't help. One false step, I thought, and I could land on one of those bombs below, and that didn't bear thinking about.

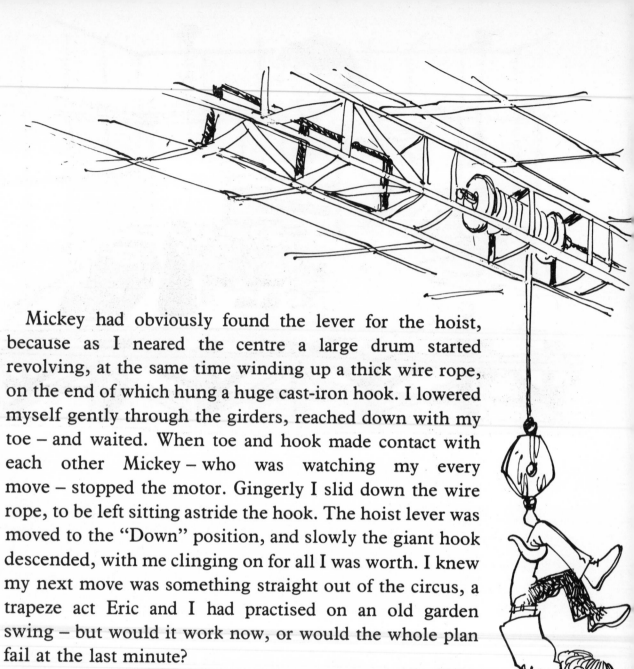

Mickey had obviously found the lever for the hoist, because as I neared the centre a large drum started revolving, at the same time winding up a thick wire rope, on the end of which hung a huge cast-iron hook. I lowered myself gently through the girders, reached down with my toe – and waited. When toe and hook made contact with each other Mickey – who was watching my every move – stopped the motor. Gingerly I slid down the wire rope, to be left sitting astride the hook. The hoist lever was moved to the "Down" position, and slowly the giant hook descended, with me clinging on for all I was worth. I knew my next move was something straight out of the circus, a trapeze act Eric and I had practised on an old garden swing – but would it work now, or would the whole plan fail at the last minute?

With care and difficulty I swung both legs over the hook and slowly lowered myself till I was hanging upside down.

It was now or never. Fortunately for me, everyone down below was too busy to look upwards, including the Baron, who was still arguing with the Works Manager over Barbara's fate. Barbara herself seemed quite unperturbed. She sat drumming her fingers on the side of the car and staring into space.

It was through that space that I descended. The look on her face was difficult to judge, as it was upside down to me – but I've no doubt it was one of amazement.

Mickey worked miracles with the crane controls and placed me directly above her. Struggling a bit, I took Eric's sticky braces out of my shirt, where I'd stuffed them, held on to the back strap and let the two front ones dangle down. They were just within Barbara's grasp and she grabbed them.

"Come *on*, Mickey, start hoisting," I said between my teeth and, as though he could read my mind, that's precisely what happened.

As I was lifted, Eric's braces stretched, taking the strain of Barbara on the other end, and slowly eased her out of the car. Once in mid-air it was the old trapeze routine again. The only trouble was that I had never practised this part before. It was with more desperation than skill that I started to swing Barbara backwards and forwards over the factory below. I could see that her eyes were closed tight. I hoped desperately that Mr Brook would guess what I was trying to do.

I needn't have bothered really, as he saw what I was up to and came out of the cab and along the girder in no time at all. Barbara was now swinging through the air with the greatest of ease, her feet heading to where Mr Brook was perched. He reached out to grab them, but just missed by a whisker. As she swung back, the Baron happened to glance up. His eyes opened wide and his monocle dropped into his even wider mouth, which let out such a roar that I could hear it in spite of all the racket below.

"Catch her this time, Mr Brook!" I shouted as I hurtled back again,
"'cause me legs won't hold on much longer!"

It was a last-effort swing, was this, and it was a good one. I swung
Barbara high enough, so all Mr Brook had to do was reach out and snatch
her to safety. As he did so, I let go of the braces and swung back,
knowing that Barbara was safe.

Now it was my turn. I concentrated on just one thing, Mr Brook's
outstretched hand. The moment our two hands made contact I slipped off
the hook and, with an almighty heave from Mr Brook, ended up sitting
on the girder next to Barbara, with no harm done. Mr Brook took
Barbara's hand and led her back to safety.

"By heck," he said, "that's started a right commotion and no mistake!"

It certainly had. Down below, uproar had broken out. Alarm bells were ringing, lights flashing and people were running about all over the place. I was a bit slow reaching the catwalk, as my legs were feeling like jelly from the strain of it all. I looked round for Mickey. There he was in the cab, not rushing at all.

"Come on, Mickey!" I yelled in alarm, "we've got to get out of here fast."

Mickey came out, taking a bottle from his pocket.

"I think I'll see if this morning's experiment works or not," he said calmly.

"By gum! You're not going to drop that, are you?" I shouted. "It'll blow us all to kingdom come!"

"That's extremely doubtful," Mickey called back, and with that he tossed the bottle into the clamour below.

We made for the trap door at top speed. The bottle cut an arc through

the air and shattered into a million pieces, spilling a strange green liquid all over the place. We crossed the roof, slid down a tree as if it was a greasy pole, and headed back to the clog.

As we paused for an instant at the hedge, Mickey shouted with glee, "It works! Look!" At that moment, wood-camouflaged doors everywhere flew open and out poured hundreds of factory workers, coughing, spluttering and holding their noses, pursued by a sort of nasty green vapour.

"Good heavens! It wasn't gas, was it?" I cried.

"No, much worse!" replied Mickey, jumping up and down with excitement. "It was the ultimate in stink bombs! Yippee!"

We sped away. Mr Brook and Barbara had just jumped aboard when we arrived, out of breath. Mickey hopped into the clog and I was about to do the same when Barbara leaned over the edge and gave me a kiss.

"There, that's for being so brave and saving my life," she said. I was dumbfounded – but Eric, true to form, broke the romantic moment.

"Come on, you two, there's no time for soppy sweetheart stuff! The engine's running and the decks are cleared for action!"

Eric stepped out of the driving seat and gave me a hand in, while Mr Brook took control and issued the final battle order.

"When I say 'Go', empty all the feathers from the pillows over the side!" he ordered.

"Eh?" said Eric.

"Now, Eric," said June, "you've done a grand job so far. Don't spoil it." And she gave him a kiss too. I think she really had a soft spot for him.

"Feathers! Girls! Treacle! . . . I'll never understand any of them," muttered Eric, clutching a pillow.

The clog rose into the air and we headed slowly towards the treacle-coated secret factory. The people running about below didn't seem to see

us, as they were too worried by the terrible smell. Mr Brook gave the order: "Go feathers!"

As we shook the pillows over the edge a flurry of feathers floated down like snowflakes. All but a few landed smack on the factory. They stuck fast, covering it from one end to the other.

"Doesn't that look pretty!" said June. "Just like an iced cake. I think I'll try one of those next."

Eric's face was a picture of disbelief.

"It stands out like a sore thumb," said Mr Brook, looking back, "and that's the whole idea."

He banked the clog round to the west, and with a touch of the throttle we accelerated like a bullet from a gun into the darkening sky.

"How long do you think that smell will keep everyone out of there?" asked Mr Brook.

"Three hours at least," answered Mickey, who was busy calculating our homeward course.

"Excellent! Our bombers can get here in no time at all. They certainly won't be able to miss that target, and there'll be nobody inside to get hurt," said Mr Brook.

"Shall I break radio silence now?" asked Eric, already donning earphones and fiddling with the dials of our crackling radio.

"Yes. Just send them our codeword 'Sore Thumb'," replied Mr Brook.

Eric gave the codeword, then pressed the earphones hard against his ears and listened intently. He grinned broadly and said, "They got it, Mr Brook. Their message reads: 'We're on our way!'" And with that we sat back and relaxed for the first time that day.

We were a silent crew flying back in the gathering dusk. From the glow of Mr Brook's pipe I looked round at the different expressions. There was June – dreaming of a recipe for an iced cake; Mickey, thinking about his next experiment; Barbara, assuring herself that she would never speak to strange men ever again; and Eric, definitely worrying about what his mum would say, as he'd missed his tea. And me – well, I was wondering what troubles we'd be in and out of on our next trip.

"Ah, well, at least Mrs Brook will be making a rice pudding for tomorrow," I said, thinking aloud.

"Tomorrow?" said Mr Brook, drawing deeply on his pipe and letting the smoke drift off into the cold evening air. "Tomorrow never comes."

And of course Mr Brook was always right.